Meg Mackintosh

and

The Case of the Curious Whale Watch

A Solve-It-Yourself Mystery

by Lucinda Landon

Little, Brown and Company
Boston   Toronto   London

First Edition

Library of Congress Cataloging-in-Publication Data
Landon, Lucinda.
Meg Mackintosh and the case of the curious whale watch.

Summary: On a whale watch, Meg tries to solve a puzzling case
involving a stolen treasure map. The reader is asked to solve the
mystery before Meg, using clues found in the text and illustrations.
[1. Mystery and detective stories. 2. Buried treasure—Fiction.
3. Literary recreations] I. Title.
PZ7.L231735Mc 1987   [Fic]   87-2748
ISBN 0-316-51362-8

10   9   8   7   6   5   4

Joy Street Books are published
by Little, Brown and Company (Inc.)

BP

Published simultaneously in Canada
by Little, Brown & Company (Canada) Limited

Printed in the United States of America

For Mom and Dad

"Sharks! Hammerhead sharks," said Peter. "That's what I want to see."

"It figures you'd be more interested in sharks than whales," Meg Mackintosh said to her brother, as they walked down the pier.

"This whale watch expedition is a grand idea," said Gramps. "What do whales watch, anyway?"

"*We* are going to watch *them*," said Meg, checking her binoculars. She had also brought her camera, notebook, and detective kit — just in case.

"The captain of the boat is quite famous," Gramps went on. "When he's not running whale watches, he's searching for a long-lost treasure that was buried by pirates in the 1800s, or so the story goes."

1

"Pirates?" said Peter.

"Lost treasure?" said Meg. "Sounds like a mystery!"

Meg, Peter, Gramps, and Skip boarded the *Albatross*.

"Welcome aboard!"
boomed a hearty voice.
"I'm Captain Caleb
Quinn.

"That's my mate,
Jasper, helping the
other passengers.

2

"There's a Mrs. Clarissa Maxwell and her nephew, Anthony.

and a young student named Carlos de Christopher.

"And a nice old gentleman, Mr. Oliver Morley,

"That's Dr. Peck, Dr. Susan Peck, a marine biologist. I guess we're all here. OK, Jasper, cast off."

3

"Are you really searching for a lost treasure?" Meg asked the captain, as they headed out to sea.

"I have an old treasure map. I'll show it to you," the captain offered. He went up to the pilothouse and returned with the map. The other passengers gathered around.

"My great-great-uncle got it from a sailor in New Zealand many years ago; he sent it to his brother, and it was passed down through the family until it got to me. Here it is, still in the original envelope.

He sent this scrimshaw, too. It's a carving of a whale on a whale's tooth."

"Did you ever find the treasure?" Meg asked.

"Never did. In all these years, no one has figured out where it is. Well, on with the whale watch. I'll lock this back up. Come on, Peter, you can help me steer."

"The treasure must be worth a lot of money," said Peter, as he followed the captain up to the pilot-house.

"I'll bet it's worth millions!" said Carlos.

"I could *use* millions," said Anthony. "Don't tell Auntie, but I'm broke if my horse doesn't win at the track today."

"That map should be destroyed," Dr. Peck said to Mr. Morley. "Those treasure hunters are always digging up the environment."

"The map looked quite authentic," replied Mr. Morley. "But I doubt the captain will ever find the treasure."

"Just think," Mrs. Maxwell said wistfully, "all those gems just sitting there."

"I wish I could solve the mystery for Captain Quinn," said Meg. She noticed Mr. Morley's magnifying glass. "Are you a detective?" she asked.

"Oh, no. Not me," said Mr. Morley.

"Thar she blows!" yelled Gramps.

Gramps was right. In the distance, a whale spouted water. Then more whales came to the surface for air.

"Whales travel in groups called pods. In the spring they migrate north to cooler waters," explained the captain. He had turned off the engines and come down from the pilothouse to point out the different whales.

Meg took photographs with her instant camera and jotted in her notebook. "We're studying whales in school," she said to Anthony.

"They're just a bunch of big fish. I only came along for the ride," he replied and stretched out to sunbathe.

"Whales aren't big fish," Meg corrected him. "They're mammals."

"And they'll be extinct if we don't protect them," Dr. Peck added. "I'm researching their migratory patterns. I was just awarded a grant."

"*My* grant money might be cut," grumbled Carlos. "Then I wouldn't be able to return to college."

Mrs. Maxwell was busier filing her fingernails than watching the whales. "May I put my purse up in the pilothouse for safekeeping?" she asked the captain.

"If you like," Captain Quinn answered. "But hurry, so you don't miss anything."

In a few minutes Mrs. Maxwell returned, and seconds later the captain let out a shout. "Look! There's a finback whale!" he exclaimed. "It's one of the largest and fastest whales. They can grow to be seventy feet long and weigh as much as sixty-five tons."

Dr. Peck ran up to the pilothouse to take photos.

Peter had a telephoto lens, too. "I should get some great shots," he said to Meg. "Much better than that little instant camera of yours."

Meg ignored Peter and went over to Gramps and Mr. Morley.

"I'm hoping to retire soon," Meg overheard Mr.

Morley say. "A few investments would help."

"I hate to cut this short," said Gramps, "but I'm feeling a bit seasick. I think I'll go in the cabin and lie down."

Meanwhile, Meg noticed Jasper slipping into a lifeboat with one of Peter's comic books. "Do you help the captain hunt for the treasure?" she asked.

"Never have," Jasper answered. "But I wouldn't mind finding that treasure myself. I'd never have to get on a boat again."

Suddenly, Mrs. Maxwell shrieked, "Look how they jump in the air!"

Albatross

"That's called breaching," said Captain Quinn. "Some say the whales leap out of the water like that to try to scratch the barnacles off their skin."

Dr. Peck came down from the pilothouse, and Carlos went up to use the telescope. Then he returned to the deck to see some whales that had come quite close to the boat.

"I've already shot three rolls of film," said Peter, as he reloaded his camera. "What time is it, anyway?"

"It's exactly eleven-forty," answered Mr. Morley, flicking his pocket watch open and shut.

"Quick! On the other side!" yelled Peter, aiming his camera. "SHARK FINS!"

Everyone raced through the passenger cabin to the port side of the boat.

"It's not a shark," said Dr. Peck. "It's a humpback whale and her calf. The calf stays with the mother, feeding and learning, for about a year, during which the mother is quite protective of the calf."

"Watch! She's fluking her tail!" exclaimed Meg. "Everyone over here. Let me take your picture with the whales in the background."

"You're blocking my sun," complained Anthony, as Meg was snapping the picture.

"No, it's a storm — and it's moving in fast," said Captain Quinn, observing the clouds. "Looks like a doozy of a nor'easter. Everybody inside, it's going to get rough. And where's that mate of mine?"

Albatross

Inside the cabin, Gramps was still asleep on the bench. Captain Quinn went to the pilothouse to start up the engines. They could hear the rain begin.

"Dr. Peck is missing," worried Mrs. Maxwell. "Where is she?"

"That's not all that's missing!" said the captain, bursting back into the cabin. "My treasure map is gone! Somebody broke into the strongbox in the pilothouse and stole it. It's got to be one of you!"

The passengers looked at each other in silence. Then the cabin door blew open and in came Dr. Peck. She was drenched.

"Where were you?" said Anthony.

"*She* was in the pilothouse earlier," said Peter. "I saw her."

"I've been on the deck observing the whales," snapped Dr. Peck. "Not that it's any of your business."

"What's all the noise about?" grumbled Gramps, rubbing his eyes.

While Captain Quinn told Gramps and Dr. Peck what had happened, Meg grabbed her knapsack and darted up to the pilothouse to inspect the scene of the crime.

The padlock on the strongbox had been broken. A handkerchief and some broken pieces of metal lay nearby. Meg got out her magnifying glass to examine the clues. Then she took a photograph.

WHAT CAN YOU DEDUCE
FROM THE SCENE OF THE CRIME?

"That's Mrs. Maxwell's handkerchief," said Peter. "It's got 'CM' on it, and the captain said that her first name is Clarissa. And those are pieces of a nail file. I saw her filing her nails, too."

"Sure it's my hankie and my nail file!" cried Mrs. Maxwell. "Someone must have taken them from my purse."

"Or maybe you just wanted it to look that way," said Carlos.

"I didn't steal that old map," she answered defiantly.

"Let me examine the padlock," said Peter. "I might be able to tell if it was broken by a left-handed or right-handed person."

"Is anything else missing, Captain Quinn?" Meg asked.

"No . . . that's it," replied the captain.

"Don't worry, Captain," Peter said confidently. "I'll find that map if I have to search everywhere and everyone. I *am* the president of my Detective Club. By the way, is there any reward?"

Meg rolled her eyes. But she knew Peter was serious about solving the mystery. If I'm going to solve this, she thought to herself, I'd better do it fast — before Peter does and before we get back to shore.

"What time is it?" Meg asked Mr. Morley.

"Sorry, I don't know. My watch is jammed shut," he answered.

Meg took out her notebook and began to make a list of all the suspects and their possible motives. Before long, she realized it wouldn't be easy to spot the thief.

WHY NOT?

Just about everybody aboard the *Albatross* had a motive!

Meg was still looking over her list of suspects when Peter burst into the pilothouse. "That mate Jasper has been sneaking around all morning," he said to Meg. "I bet he had something to do with the theft."

"Jasper's had a million chances to steal the map," replied Meg. "Why would he pick today?"

"Then what about Carlos?" Peter pointed his finger accusingly. "Weren't you in the pilothouse using the captain's telescope?"

"Everything was fine when I left there," Carlos protested.

"Well, someone definitely stole my hankie and nail file from my purse," said Mrs. Maxwell, who was still clutching Anthony's hand.

"But nothing else was missing?" asked Meg. "Your wallet and all of your money are still there?"

"Yes . . . it's all there," she answered, somewhat flustered.

"What about you, Anthony?" Peter looked at him. "It's no secret that you need some cash . . . or is it?"

"Oh, no, not my little Anthony," said Mrs. Max-well. "He'd never steal a thing."

"Just like that humpback protecting her calf," said Meg quietly.

"Humpback? What are you talking about?" said Mr. Morley.

"What about *you*, Meg?" Mrs. Maxwell interrupted. "You've been snooping around about that treasure map all day!"

"Meg wouldn't steal the map," Peter defended her. "She'd rather solve mysteries than cause them."

"Well, I'd be careful if I were you," warned Anthony. "Playing detective could get you into trouble."

Now I *have* to solve the case, Meg thought to herself, before I become a suspect! She thought hard. It's the timing that's important. The thief must have struck after the captain left the pilothouse and came down to point out the whales. Where was everyone after that?

Meg thought back to what had happened. She decided to draw a picture of the boat and, with the help of her photos, map out where everyone had been.

Meanwhile, the storm was getting rough. All of the passengers were huddled in the cabin, except Peter, who was timing how long it would take to run up the steps to the pilothouse, break into the strongbox, and then run back down. Captain Quinn and Jasper were busy guiding the *Albatross* through the dense fog.

"How's it going?" Gramps asked Meg, peering over her shoulder. He still looked a bit green.

"Well, it's hard to say," said Meg. "Peter thinks the nail file and handkerchief point to Mrs. Maxwell. But I doubt she would leave her tools at the scene of the crime. I think Carlos was in the pilothouse last, but it's possible someone slipped up after him. I'm still trying to figure out everyone's alibi. I also have some instant photos I took. They might show something," she confided in him.

"Let's see," said Gramps. "Nice shot of me and Skip."

Mr. Morley was sitting nearby. "I'd check out that Dr. Peck if I were you," he whispered. "She's been acting very suspiciously."

Peter overheard them and decided to get to Dr. Peck first. A wave pitched the *Albatross* sharply; Peter knocked into her and was able to dump her camera bag on the floor. The top of a lens case came off and out fell . . .

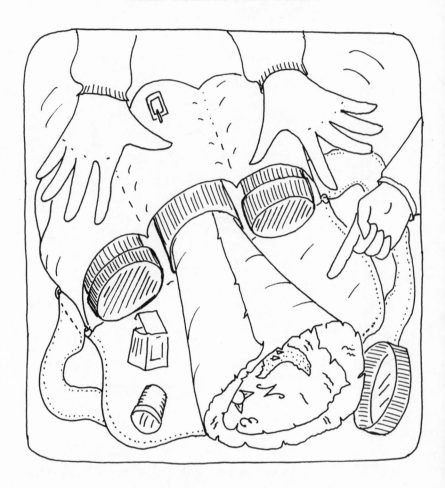

"What have we here?" said Peter triumphantly. "Looks like I've found our crook. You can forget all about your little deductions, Meg-O. The case of the missing treasure map is *closed.*"

"What? How did that get there?" exclaimed Dr. Peck. "I didn't take that map. I never touched it!"

"Wait until the Detective Club hears about this," boasted Peter, as he handed the map over to Captain Quinn.

"I knew she did it," said Anthony. "Scientists are creepy."

"She said she thought treasure maps should be destroyed," said Mr. Morley. "I guess she really meant it."

"Is it the same map?" asked Carlos. "She could have copied it."

"That's my map, all right," said the captain. "I'm going to have to tell the police about this, but first we have to get through this storm."

"You're all wrong!" cried Dr. Peck. "I didn't steal the map!"

I believe her, Meg thought to herself. Something doesn't make sense. Meg looked over her drawings and photos to try to figure out what.

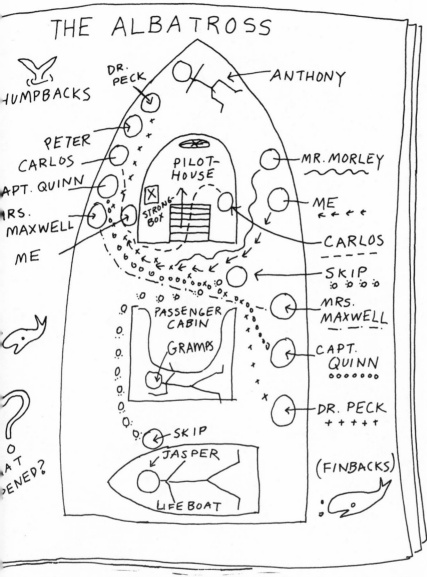

After a moment, Meg knew she was right. The case was *not* closed. Dr. Peck couldn't have stolen the map.

WHY NOT?

"Dr. Peck did go up to the pilothouse to take photographs," Meg explained to Gramps. She had pulled him out on deck, out of earshot of the others. "But Carlos went up there to use the telescope *after* she did, and he said everything was fine. Dr. Peck was on the deck with the rest of us until the storm. I remember talking to her then, and she's in the group photo I took."

"But if Dr. Peck didn't do it," said Gramps, "how did the map get in her camera bag?"

"Maybe somebody else — I don't know who — took the map and then planted it on Dr. Peck. You know, like a red herring, to throw us off the track," Meg replied.

"You mean they figured out where the treasure was and then ditched the map on Dr. Peck?" Gramps scratched his head.

"That would be pretty fast thinking," said Meg. "Four generations of Quinns haven't been able to find the treasure. But why would someone steal the map only to return it?" Meg decided to have another look at the map. She headed up to the pilothouse to talk to Captain Quinn.

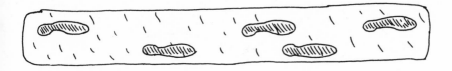

"This whole thing is as foggy to me as that weather out there," said Captain Quinn, as he leaned over the steering wheel and gazed out to sea. "I don't understand why a professor of ocean life would want to steal my old map. I suspect the gold and gems are worth a tidy sum, but I've logged a lot of hours looking for that treasure — it won't come easy."

"I don't think Dr. Peck *did* steal the map," Meg said, and explained why. "Could I see the map again?"

"Help yourself," said the captain. "It's back in the strongbox."

Meg took out the map, then noticed the scrimshaw and took it out, too. "At least the thief didn't bother with this," she said.

Meg studied the map and scrimshaw with her magnifying glass, and went over her notes and photographs again. After a while she realized that, although Peter had found the treasure map, something else was missing.

WHAT?

The envelope. They'd found the map, but not the envelope it came in. Where was it? And what difference could an old envelope make? Meg wondered.

Suddenly there was a loud CLUNK. The lights in the cabin blinked and went out. The engine was dead; the *Albatross* drifted in the storm.

"Jumping jellyfish!" yelled the captain. "Don't worry, Meg. I'll go down below and help Jasper get her going again. You stay here."

Meg could hear the other passengers scurrying about in the cabin below.

"What's happened to the power?" asked Carlos nervously.

"We're not going to sink, are we?" said Anthony.

"Are we stranded with a dangerous criminal aboard?" exclaimed Mrs. Maxwell.

"I'm not dangerous . . . and I'm not a criminal," insisted Dr. Peck. "This is absurd!"

"I found the treasure map on you," said Peter. "That's pretty strong proof."

"Where *is* the map?" asked Mr. Morley. "Someone may try to steal it again while the lights are out."

Meg clutched the map tightly, but what she was really thinking about was the envelope. In a moment, she figured out what had happened to it — and suddenly the whole case fell into place. She ran down to the cabin.

"Listen, everybody. Dr. Peck *didn't* steal the map.
I know who did!"

WHO?

"Mr. Morley!" Meg announced. "He stole the treasure map!"

"What? Not I! What would I want with a worthless old map?" asked Mr. Morley.

"Nothing," Meg agreed. "But you did want the stamp on the envelope the map was sent in. You noticed that it was very old and valuable — you even had your magnifying glass and stamp-collecting book to verify it. You waited until Captain Quinn was out of the pilothouse and everyone else was busy watching the whales, then you snuck in and stole it. You took the treasure map to throw us off the track, and you planted it on Dr. Peck to make her look guilty. You figured that no one would ever miss the envelope or stamp."

Mr. Morley turned red as a lobster. "You have no proof. You're just playing detective," he protested. "Why, I've had no opportunity to take the map, even if I wanted to!"

"That's not true," said Meg. "You did have an opportunity."

WHEN?

"When we all ran to the port side of the boat to see
the whales, you weren't there," Meg explained. "My
photos prove it — you're not in the group shot. And
when I mentioned that Mrs. Maxwell and Anthony
were acting like a humpback whale and her calf, you
didn't know what I was talking about — because you
weren't there when we saw them. You were in the
pilothouse stealing the map and the envelope.
Anthony was sunbathing. Jasper was reading Peter's
comic books in the lifeboat. Gramps was asleep in

the cabin and didn't see you. The rest of us were on deck. You took Mrs. Maxwell's nail file to break the padlock and used her handkerchief to wipe off your fingerprints. Then you rolled up the map and stuffed it into Dr. Peck's camera-lens case, which she had left on the bench in the cabin. I think you ripped the stamp off the envelope and threw the envelope overboard to be rid of it. And I think I know where you put the stamp, too."

WHERE?

"I bet it's in your pocket watch," Meg continued. "At eleven-forty, you snapped it open and told Peter what time it was. That was before the theft. But afterward, when I asked you the time, you said your watch was jammed shut. Ten-to-one you quickly hid the stamp inside to keep it safe and dry."

"This is absolutely ridiculous," Mr. Morley insisted. "I refuse to listen to any more of these wild accusations. This amateur sleuth has clearly invented this story for her own amusement."

Captain Quinn stepped forward. "I think we'd better see your watch," he said. "If Meg's theory is as farfetched as you say, surely you won't mind if we have a look."

Peter added, "If you didn't do it, you have nothing to hide!" The others agreed. They stared at Mr. Morley as he fumbled for his pocket watch. Meg held her breath.

Mr. Morley scowled as he handed the pocket watch over to the captain.

Sure enough, the stamp was there. Just as Meg had suspected.

"I never thought you'd miss one little stamp," groaned Mr. Morley. "But such a valuable little stamp . . . an 1855 New Zealand. I can't believe I let it slip through my fingers."

"He was going to let me be arrested!" cried Dr. Peck.

There was another clunk and the engine started up. The lights flickered back on.

"I got her going again, Cap!" shouted Jasper.

"The police will take care of Mr. Morley when we get back to shore," said Captain Quinn. "It's nice to have a valuable stamp, but I'm really just happy to have my old treasure map back — even though I still don't know where the treasure is."

"But that's not all!" exclaimed Meg. "I think I can help you with that, too."

HOW?

Meg got out her magni-
fying glass and the
scrimshaw. "If you look at
the scrimshaw carefully,
the whale looks like the island on the treasure map.

And if you turn the map this way, it resembles a
whale. I noticed it when I was examining the clues.

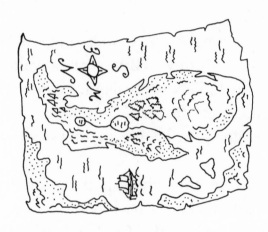

I think the sailor gave your great-great-uncle both
the map and the scrimshaw so they would comple-
ment each other in telling the location of the treasure. So, if someone stole the map, they still couldn't
figure out where the treasure was. You need *both* of
them to find it.

"See," Meg continued. "The eye on the scrim-shaw whale looks like an 'X.' I bet that 'X' marks the spot on the island where you should look for the treasure."

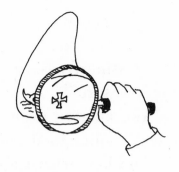

The captain's jaw dropped in surprise.

"Now that I see it, it makes perfect sense," he said. "As simple as putting one plus one together. In fact, I think I recognize the spot . . . it's at . . . wait a minute. I want to be the one to find it first. Thanks, Meg!"

"I guess you really solved two mysteries at once," Gramps said to Meg a few weeks later. "The Case of the Missing Treasure Map and The Case of the Missing Treasure."

"You amazed even me," Peter admitted. "But I did get some great photos of the whales."

"And look what Captain Quinn gave me for solving the mystery," said Meg. "A whale watch!"